♡ The Nature Club ♡

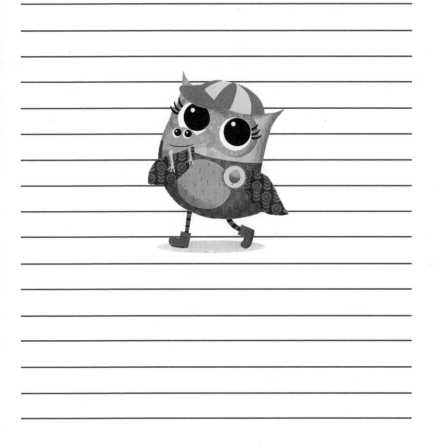

Read more
OWL DIARIES books!

1. Eva's Treetop Festival
2. Eva Sees a Ghost
3. A Woodland Wedding
4. Eva and the New Owl
5. Warm Hearts Day

6. Baxter Is Missing
7. The Wildwood Bakery
8. Eva and the Lost Pony
9. Eva's Big Sleepover
10. Trip to the Pumpkin Farm

11. Eva's Big Sleepover
12. Eva's Campfire Adventure
13. Eva in the Spotlight
14. Eva at the Beach
15. Eva's New Pet

16. Get Well, Eva
17. Eva in the Band
18. The Nature Club
19. Eva for President

OWL DIARIES

♥ The Nature Club ♥

Rebecca
Elliott

SCHOLASTIC INC.

For Clementine, who always loved
a walk in the woods. X. — R.E.

Special thanks to Collaborate Agency for
their contributions to this book.

Library of Congress Cataloging-in-Publication Data
Names: Elliott, Rebecca, author, illustrator.
Title: The nature club / Rebecca Elliott.
Description: First edition | New York : Branches/Scholastic, Inc., 2023. |
Series: Owl diaries ; 18 | Audience: Ages 5–7. | Audience: Grades K–2. |
Summary: When Mrs. Featherbottom places Eva in a different club from
Lucy and Hailey, Eva misses her best friends, but she learns new things
about her classmates, and discovers that someone in her
club is missing a friend, too.
Identifiers: LCCN 2022041071 (print) | LCCN 2022041072 (ebook) |
ISBN 9781338745467 (paperback) | ISBN 9781338745474 (library binding) |
ISBN 9781338745481 (ebk)
Subjects: CYAC: Owls–Fiction. | Best friends–Fiction. |
Friendship–Fiction. | Nature–Fiction. | Schools–Fiction. |
Diaries--Fiction. | BISAC: JUVENILE FICTION / Readers / Chapter Books |
JUVENILE FICTION / Animals / Birds | LCGFT: Animal fiction.
Classification: LCC PZ7.E45812 Nat 2023 (print) | LCC PZ7.E45812 (ebook)
| DDC [Fic]–dc23
LC record available at https://lccn.loc.gov/2022041071

ISBN 978-1-338-74547-4 (hardcover) / ISBN 978-1-338-74546-7 (paperback)

10 9 8 7 6 5 4 3 2 1   22 23 24 25 26

Printed in China   62
First edition, May 2023

Edited by Katie Carella and Alli Brydon
Book design by Marissa Asuncion

♡ Table of Contents ♡

1 Nature Day   1
2 Mission: Save the Planet!   12
3 Hop In!   23
4 HOO Will Win?   36
5 Best Feathery Friends Forever   49
6 Together Again   55
7 The Grand Prize   64

♡ Nature Day ♡

Sunday

Hello, Diary!
It's me, Eva. Next Saturday is Nature Day! There is going to be a party at the Old Oak Tree to celebrate the planet.

<u>I love</u>:

Nature!

Leafy trees

Finding bugs outside

Splashing in
puddles

Swapping . . . instead of shopping!

Planting seeds

Recycling boxes

The word <u>Earth</u>

<u>I DO NOT love</u>:

Litter

Seeing nature
get hurt

Crashing into
leafy trees

Finding bugs
inside

Holes in my
rain boots

Missing my BFF

Forgetting to
water my plants

The word
pollution

This is my **WING-CREDIBLE** family.

Dad

Mom

Me

Baby Mo

Humphrey

And these are my pets, Baxter the bat and Acorn the flying squirrel. They love nature, too!

Being an owl is **FLAPPY-FABULOUS**.

We're awake at night instead of during the day.

We can stretch, yawn, and comb our heads.

We can swim!

The biggest owl in the world has a
wingspan as wide as a couch!

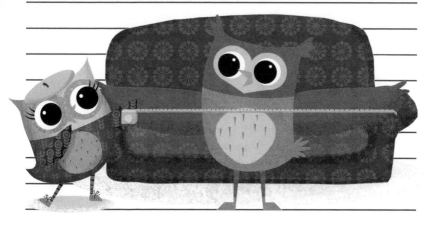

My address is 11 Woodpine Avenue, Treetopolis, Planet Earth. My BFF (**BEST FEATHERY FRIEND**), Lucy, lives next door.

We go to Treetop Owlementary
School. Here's our class:

Sue
Lilly
Mrs.
Lucy
Featherbottom
Macy
Me
Hailey
Zac
George
Carlos
Jacob
Kiera
Zara

ANYHOOT, I can't
wait for tomorrow —
because it's one day
closer to Nature Day!

♥ Mission: Save the Planet! ♥

At school this week, we'll be learning about nature. Tonight, Mrs. Featherbottom talked about how important it is to love and protect our planet.

12

Then she announced a cool project.

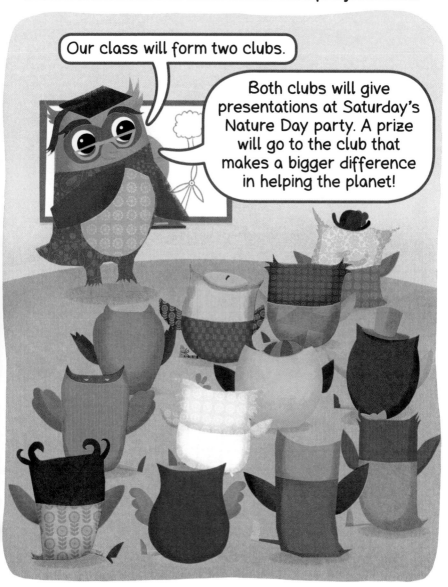

Our class will form two clubs.

Both clubs will give presentations at Saturday's Nature Day party. A prize will go to the club that makes a bigger difference in helping the planet!

We were all buzzing with excitement.

I love being part of a club!

Me too!

Let's all be in one together.

Sue, would you like to be in my club?

Wow! That would be nice, Zara.

But then Mrs. Featherbottom said something surprising.

I wanted to work with my BFFs, Lucy and Hailey. But I was also excited about being in a new club.

In the end, we agreed we would all be the leaders.

To help the planet, we decided to start with our home – the forest.

After school, Lucy came over to my tree house. I told her about our club's goal.

That's super! We're the Recycle Club. We're going to show how fun it is to reuse and recycle.

Owlsome! Should we "recycle" these blueberries into milkshakes?

Yes!

We made yummy milkshakes!

I'm sad I'm not in the same club as Lucy, but at least we can still hang out after school. Time for bed, Diary . . . I have a planet to save tomorrow!

3

♡ Hop In! ♡

School was a **HOOT** tonight! First,
Mrs. Featherbottom gave us club hats!

Then we made club badges. What do you think, Diary?!

Next, Nature Club made a to-do list:

1. Plant flower seeds

2. Make posters about nature

PROTECT OUR PLANET!

3. Build a bug hotel

BUG HOTEL

4. Create wild art

But we couldn't agree on what we should do first!

Our nature walk was **FLAPERRIFIC**!
We discovered bugs. And we collected
twigs, leaves, and pinecones to make
our bug hotel and wild art.

At the river, we saw lots of frogs!

What is a frog's favorite candy?

I don't know, Macy. What?

Lolli-HOPS!

Then George noticed something **OWLFUL**. A frog was stuck in some trash!

Jacob freed the frog! Then –

He fell into the river!

The water's warm. Jump in!

We swam for a while. Then the Recycle Club flew by.

We left to fly back to school while the Recycle Club stayed to collect more trash.

Sorry we can't hang out.

It's okay, Eva!

See you soon!

Back at school, we planted flower seeds in small pots. It was messy and fun!

We'll plant these outside when they're big enough.

Wouldn't it be cool to have our own garden?

Totally!

<u>Before we knew it, school was over.</u>

I'm tired!

Me too! I'm going to just chill when I get home!

No time for rest if we want to win the Nature Day prize! We need to make posters.

I was hoping to see my BFFs tonight!

Sorry, there's work to do!

<u>I was making</u>
<u>posters when Lucy</u>
<u>and Hailey called.</u>

Want to hang out, Eva?

I can't. Sue wants us to make posters tonight!

Oh well. So how is being in a club with Sue?

It's okay. She seems extra grumpy, but I think she just wants to win.

And I miss my besties!

We miss you, too!

I miss hanging out with Lucy and Hailey. But I must finish these posters because I do want to win that prize (and save the planet, of course!).

HOO Will Win?

Wednesday

Tonight, the Nature Club designed and built our bug hotel.

Buggingham Palace

- Pebbles
- Brick
- Bamboo
- Plastic Bottle
- Twigs
- Dirt
- Straw
- Wood
- Log
- Leaves

What do you think, Diary?

Mrs. Featherbottom stopped by to check on our project.

Lucy was wearing a **BEHOOTIFUL** dress made from trash — like cardboard and plastic bottles. It wasn't finished, but it looked really cool!

I thought Sue might be jealous that the other club was making clothes, since fashion is <u>her</u> passion. But she was being super nice to Zara!

We needed to stop worrying that our club wasn't as good as the Recycle Club.

As we designed our wild art, I saw that Sue looked upset.

Before we flew off to hang our posters, I asked if she was okay.

While we hung our posters around the forest, Jacob and Macy kept making me laugh.

They're so funny! How did I not know that about them?

The Recycle Club was putting up their posters, too.

Diary, Sue is feeling sad and I think it's making her act mean. I wish I could figure out why she's unhappy . . .

♡ Best Feathery Friends Forever ♡

Thursday

Mrs. Featherbottom kept yawning
while teaching tonight.

After lunch, we collected more materials for our **FLAPPY-FABULOUS** wild art. Then we started making it.

We also played around!

I realized that I've gotten to know these friends so much better being in our club this week. They're really kind and funny!

Back at home, I thought of how I still missed Lucy and Hailey. But I hoped they were having fun with their club mates, just like I was!

Then the doorbell rang.

We had the most fun ever!

I had such a **HOOTIFUL** time with my besties. How can we help Zara and Sue realize that they're best friends, too? Oh, Diary — I have an idea!

♡ Together Again ♡

Friday

At school, Mrs. Featherbottom was trying to hide something behind her back.

The Nature Club watered our seeds and finished our wild art.

Only one more night until the Nature Day party!

We brought everything to the Old Oak Tree to set up for tomorrow.

While everyone was working, I pulled Sue aside. Time to put my idea into action!

This week has been really fun. But I've missed my best friends.

Have you missed anyone, Sue?

No. And I've never had a best friend.

Well, I think Zara's been missing you. Maybe she's your best friend . . .

Really?

Then the Recycle Club arrived.

I went over to Zara.

Hey, Zara! How's it going?

It's going okay. But our recycled outfits are falling apart.

Maybe Sue can help!

I would love that! But do you think she'll want to?

Of course, Zara. You two are like best friends!

We are?

You'll see! Come with me!

Sue and Zara liked my suggestion!

Both clubs worked together to finish setting up for Nature Day.

Then we all flew home.

Great job helping Sue and Zara see what good friends they are, Eva!

Thanks!

It was so much fun working as one big group tonight!

Totally! Wait — I have an idea!

Diary, my besties and I made the best plan ever! But now I'm so tired . . .

Zzz

♡ The Grand Prize ♡

Nature Day finally arrived! Everyone in Treetopolis gathered at the Old Oak Tree to celebrate.

The mayor led us all in "The Nature Day Song."

> Owls around the earth unite
> To make our planet clean and bright.
> The earth, it needs our love a lot
> 'Cause it's the only one we've got!

Soon, it was time for our presentations.

The Recycle Club showed everyone how to reuse and recycle.

Then they put on a fashion show in their **FLAPPY-FABULOUS** outfits.

We hope you're as excited about recycling as we are!

Everyone clapped and cheered!

The Nature Club presented our bug hotel and our new seedlings.

Then we shared our wild art project!

Everyone clapped and cheered again!

Mrs. Featherbottom stepped up to the microphone next.

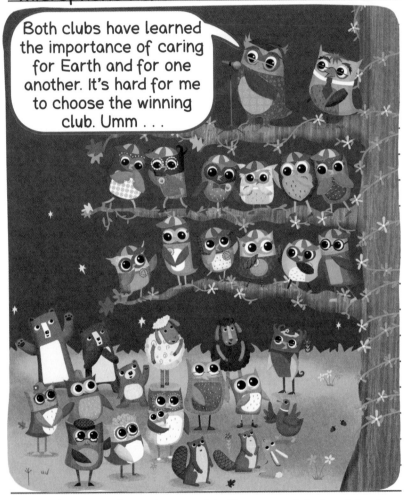

That's when Lucy, Hailey, and I decided to speak up.

Diary, I've had the BEST week! Turns out, looking after the world around you isn't just important – it's fun, too! (Especially when you work together!)

I'm so lucky to live on this **FLAPTASTIC** planet with so many great friends. That's the real prize. See you next time!

Rebecca Elliott was a lot like Eva when she was younger: She loved making things and hanging out with her best friends. Now that Rebecca is older, not much has changed — except that her best friends now include her two sons, Benjy and Toby. She still loves making things, like stories, cakes, music, and paintings. But as much as she and Eva have in common, Rebecca cannot fly or turn her head all the way around. No matter how hard she tries.

Rebecca is the author of several picture books, the young adult novel PRETTY FUNNY FOR A GIRL, and the bestselling UNICORN DIARIES and OWL DIARIES early chapter book series.

OWL DIARIES

Eva's life is a real HOOT!

Eva's class is preparing to celebrate Nature Day. Mrs. Featherbottom splits everyone into two clubs. Each club has to come up with ways to help the planet. The club that makes the **biggest** difference will win a secret prize! But Eva is not in the same club as Lucy and Hailey. Will Eva miss her friends?

Read Eva's next treetop adventure!

OWL DIARIES
♥ Eva for President ♥

Cover art © 2022 by Rebecca Elliott
Cover design by Maria Mercado and Marissa Asuncion

SCHOLASTIC
scholastic.com/branches

$5.99 US / $7.99 CAN

ISBN 978-1-338-74546-7

50599

APPEALS TO
1ST-2ND GRADERS

READING LEVEL
GRADE 2

Find more leveling information for this book at:
scholastic.com/brancheslevels

9 781338 745467

P9-BAJ-621